Jan Kjær & Merlin P. Mann

TAYNIKMA

Book 3: Tower of the Sun

D1352988

Young World Digital
MMIX

TAYNIKMA
Book 3: Tower of the Sun
(Original title: Soltårnet)

Translated by Merlin P. Mann

© Jan Kjær & Merlin P. Mann
© This edition Young World Digital Ltd, London, U.K.

ISBN 978-0-9558337-2-4
First edition

Published by:
Young World Digital Ltd • PO Box 6268 • London W1A 2HE
www.youngworlddigital.com

Printed and bound in Great Britain in 2009
by Stanley L. Hunt (Printers) Ltd, Rushden, Northants

All rights reserved. No part of this publication may be reproduced, stored in a
retrieval system, or transmitted in any form or by any means, electronic, mechanical,
photo-copying, recording or otherwise, without the prior permission of the publishers.

British Library Cataloguing in Publication Data available.

TAYNIKMA
Book 1: Master Thief
Book 2: The Rats
Book 3: Tower of the Sun
Book 4: The Lost Catacombs
Book 5: The Secret Arena
Book 6: Duel of the Clans
Book 7: Henzel's Ambush
Book 8: The Forest of Shadows
Book 9: The Fortress of Light
Book 10: The Final Battle

www.taynikma.co.uk

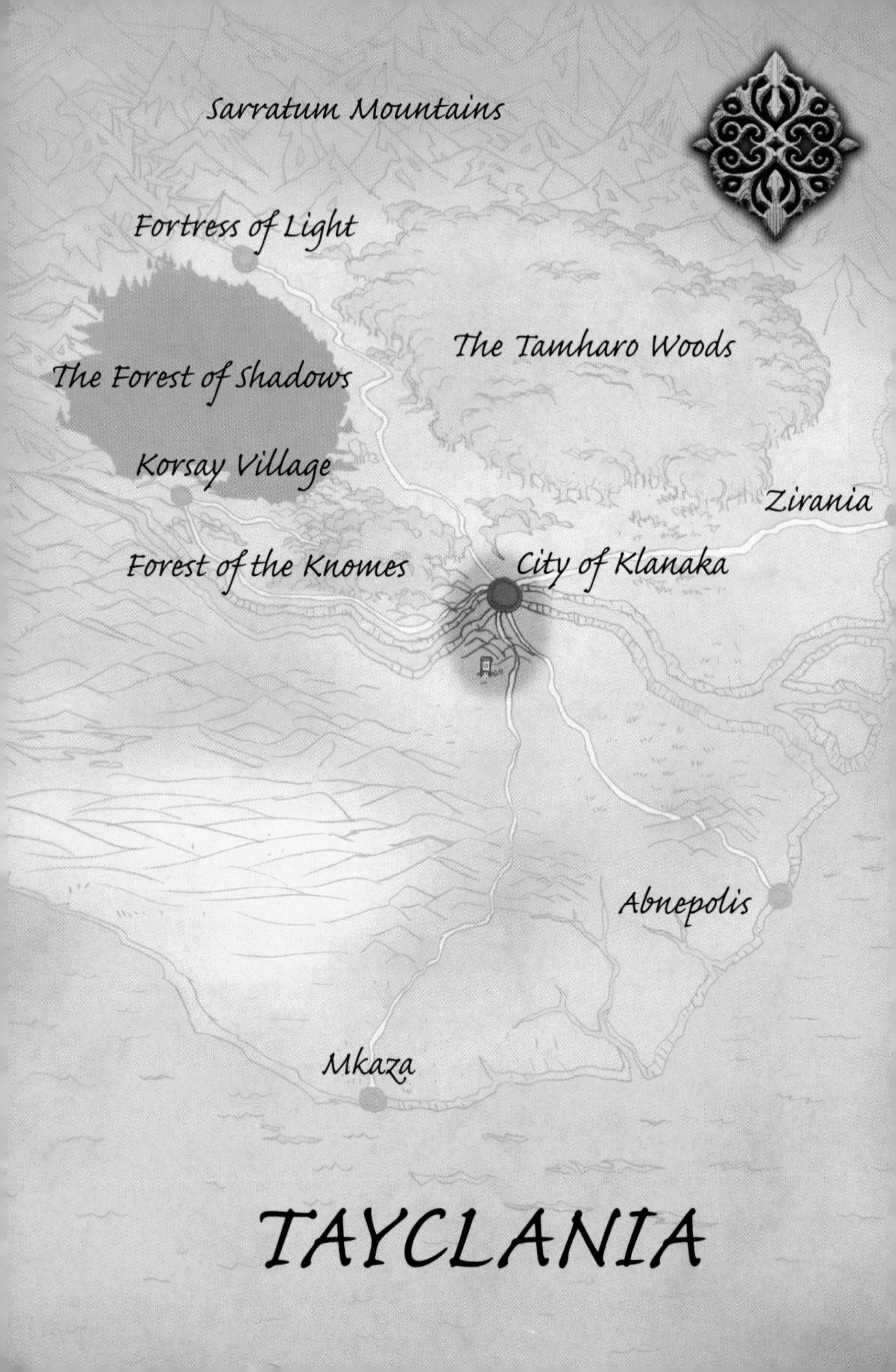

Sarratum Mountains

Fortress of Light

The Tamharo Woods

The Forest of Shadows

Korsay Village

Zirania

Forest of the Knomes

City of Klanaka

Abnepolis

Mkaza

TAYCLANIA

Tayclania

South of the mountains, north of the sea lies the land of Tayclania.

For hundreds of years it was a haven for merchants, craftsmen and scholars. The land was ruled by the four clans: The Sun, The Moon, The Mountain and The River.

Each clan had its deities and powers. The Sun Clan had the healing powers of light, the Moon Clan had the protection of shadow, the Mountain Clan had raw strength and the River Clan had wisdom.

Even though it was a land of plenty, quarrels began between the clans. Quarrels led to fights.
Fights led to war.

A treaty was signed, but few believed the four clans could rule together again.

Peace was short-lived. A sorceress murdered three champions from each clan and from their souls she created a total of 12 invincible knights: the Sentinels. Soon all of Tayclania had to bow to her rule and she became The Empress.

The clans were outlawed, the borders were closed and The Empress imposed the Law of the Sun. She declared that only by having just one deity could the land live in peace and harmony. A brief uprising was attempted by the clans but easily crushed by the Sentinels.

Soon the rule of the immortal Empress of Light will have lasted for 100 years.

KOTO

14 years old and training with Master Gekko to become a thief. He has a special ability with shadows and with his taynikma he can overcome great challenges.

MONTO

16 years old and a soldier in the army of Klanaka. His father was a hero of war, who died shortly after Monto was born. Monto is strong, loyal and is expected to follow in his father's footsteps.

CAPTAIN HENZEL

The head of the army of Klanaka, a vain and greedy man. He answers only to the Empress and her dreaded Sentinels, whose orders he reluctantly follows.

The story so far ...

Koto and his parents will lose their home unless they get 300 coins. Koto travels to the city Klanaka to sell an old  heirloom, but a gang of thieves steal it from him.

The master thief Gekko makes Koto his apprentice and teaches him all he needs to know to steal back what is his.

A lot more training ...

Koto enters the caves of the robber gang, but he quickly  realizes that a danger far greater awaits him in the deep.

But that's madness!

Despite the odds he finds the old heirloom and discovers that it holds magical powers.

 It is an ancient Taynikma. Now Koto is ready to face his true destiny!

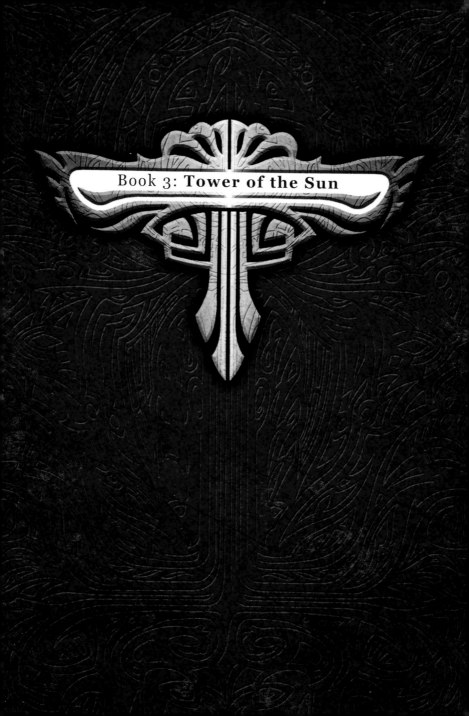

Book 3: Tower of the Sun

Monto

Lt. Lenzor!
What happened
to my uncle?

The tall officer was headed for the stables, but he stopped and turned towards Monto.

»Your uncle has disappeared,« he said with a stern face. »Now return to your duties, soldier!«

»But how did he disappear? Is anyone out looking for him?« Monto asked desperately.

»A soldier is not supposed to ask questions!« said Lt. Lenzor. Monto was about to protest, but Lenzor laid a firm hand on his shoulder.

We all know
how well your
father served
the corps!

»That gives you something to live up to, Monto! You must learn to obey the rules if you hope to be just half the soldier your father was!«

Monto nodded and bowed his head.

We're at war, Monto ...

»The people are scared. They need protection,« said Lenzor. »All was chaos before Henzel enforced the law of the Empress. Chaos and lawlessness!«

Monto caught a glimpse of the two soldiers training in the yard. One was wounded, but their master made no move to stop the ill-matched fight.

»The battle against chaos requires discipline,« said Lenzor. »No one must act on his own whims. Henzel's orders must be obeyed at all times!«

Just then the big soldier swung his dummy sword, knocking his wounded opponent to the ground.

Lack of discipline would be our downfall!

Lenzor looked Monto right in the eye. His stare was cold as ice.

Your uncle was on duty when he disappeared!

»He never had the morale of your father and I would not be surprised if he simply deserted. Like a scurvy traitor ...«

My uncle is no traitor!

The sharp pain of the whip against his cheek silenced Monto.

Do not dishonour your father's name!

»I still expect great things from you. Dismissed, soldier Monto!«

Monto stayed behind as Lenzor turned sharply and walked to the stables. He finally realised that no one would help him find out what had really happened to his uncle.

»I want to be a good soldier,« thought Monto as he rode from the castle that night heading for the barracks, where he lived. »But Father was killed serving in the corps – and now my uncle is gone! I have no family left ...«

Monto had taken the route through the potters' quarter. It was not the shortest way to the barracks, but it took him past his uncle's house, and something inside him was prodding him in that direction.

»I shouldn't be here,« thought Monto as he took a deep breath. »But I have to know ...«

... if Uncle left me a message!

Monto tied up his horse a few streets away. Soldiers could be searching the house and it would not be good for Monto to be seen here. »Stay,« Monto whispered to his horse and crept closer to the house. Not that it was much of a house. More of a shed.

Uncle had lived by himself for many years and done hardly any work on the house.

What the ...?

A burglar?

Obviously not a soldier ...

Monto pulled out his mace and the special lantern his father had given him. He walked slowly up to the house. The door had been boarded up and a Sun-insignia clearly stated that this property now belonged to the corps. Monto listened carefully. The burglar was completely silent, moving around without any light.

Monto crept into the alley and hid right by the open window. »Come on out,« thought Monto. »I have a warm welcome for you ...«

Finally a dark figure appeared on the windowsill from the inside. Someone with eyes that glowed red in the dark!

Thief!

TENE-FALANX!

Monto had no idea what hit him, and the burglar took off down the dark alley.

»You're not getting away, you fool!« yelled Monto as he got on his feet. He knew the alley was a dead end. There was no way out for the burglar.

Monto looked down the alley, but he didn't see anyone. Even though it was dark he ought be able to spot someone hiding.

Monto looked around, examining every possible hiding place. But there was only the silent darkness.

»You're a clever sneak,« mumbled Monto, as he got out his small lantern.

A blinding light as strong as a sunbeam pierced through the darkness.

ARRRH!

Put that light away!

Got you!

The burglar was obviously blinded by the light from the crystal, but he was still trying to get away.

Monto grabbed hold of his leg and jerked. The confused burglar fell flat on the ground and Monto was on him in a flash.

»What were you doing in my uncle's house?!« snarled Monto, raising his fist.

»Calm down, you cave-troll!« gasped the burglar and looked Monto straight in the eyes. »I'm trying to save your uncle, blast it!«

Monto gave the young thief a bewildered look. »What do you mean? Who are you?«

»My name is Koto,« said the burglar and pushed Monto away to get back on his feet.

Put that crystal away!

Where did you get that?

»My father got it from Captain Henzel. It was made to find thieving rascals like you!«

»I wasn't here to steal anything,« said Koto. »I'm looking for clues that could lead to your uncle!«

Monto grabbed Koto by the neck. »What do you want from my uncle? Speak up!«

»Back off, will you! Blockhead!« said Koto. »My master, Gekko, wants to talk to him ...«

»About what?«

»Gekko is looking for the remains of the rebel clans. Your uncle has been a spy for them for years ...«

My uncle is no traitor!

»No, he's NOT a traitor! He's a rebel!« said Koto. »He wants to bring down the rule of Henzel. But it seems his cover was blown ...«

Monto gritted his teeth so hard it sounded like grinding bones. He pushed Koto hard up against the wall.

»Are you lying to me, you thief?!«

»No!« replied Koto. »He was set up. The corps has captured him!

If you want to see your uncle again, you'd better let me go!

Monto stood petrified for a moment, but he didn't let go of Koto. Then he pulled him out into the street. »I'm a soldier,« said Monto. »It is my duty to put scum like you behind bars!«

Monto dragged him to his horse and quickly tied up his hands.

»You're making a big mistake!« said Koto, but Monto simply slung him onto the horse like a sack.

The Interrogation

Monto had only waited shortly in the interrogation chamber when Captain Henzel himself arrived.

This had to be more than a regular burglar. Normally Captain Henzel would never attend the interrogation of a petty thief.

Henzel walked slowly over to Koto with an evil grin on his face.

»I've been looking for this weasel for some time now,« said Henzel. »A barbarian spy seeking to destroy our great country. What's your name, scoundrel?«

»My name is Koto and I'm neither a spy nor a barbarian!« said Koto. »I come from the village of Corsay, and I was simply trying to sell ...«

LIAR!

»You work for the rebel clans! Where else would you get a nikma?« Henzel pointed to the table where the strange artifact that had been on Koto's arm was lying.

»I got the taynikma from my parent!« snapped Koto. »I don't know where the clans are, but if I ever find them I will gladly join the rebellion and help bring you down, Henzel!«

The captain's pale face turned grey and his breathing grew heavy with rage. Then he pulled out a nasty-looking tool with a sharp, metal claw.

»You will tell me the way to the secret city of the clans,« whispered Henzel. »And after that you will beg me to put an end to your suffering ...«

Monto was shocked to see Henzel walk over to Koto with the devilish tool.

Koto gritted his teeth.

Forget it,
Henzel!

»Even if I knew the way ...« he continued. »... I would never tell you, you dimwit!«

»I will break every bone in your body, unless you start talking,« sneered Henzel. »You will tell me everything, pathetic little boy. But do please resist me. I love the sound of pain!«

A terrible shriek sounded from Koto, as Henzel grabbed his chest with the metal claw.

Stop, Captain!

You'll kill
him!

Did
you speak,
soldier?

Monto looked around. There was only one other
soldier in the chamber and he seemed not to care that
Henzel was about to torture a defenceless boy younger
than Monto. Maybe even kill him ...

»He's just a boy,« said Monto, but Henzel just gave
him a freezing stare.

»A soldier is not supposed to ask questions!« said
Henzel, taking a set of knuckledusters from the table.
»Now question the traitor instead.«

That is, unless
you want to disobey
a direct order ...

»And be punished like this thief!«

Monto tried to remain calm as he looked at the knuckledusters. Out of the corner of his eye he could see Koto writhing with pain. Monto doubted if the boy would survive such a beating, but the other soldier stood ready to thrust his spear into Monto.

You are either with us or against us!

Which will it be?

Monto hesitantly reached for the knuckleduster. Henzel smiled and gave it to him.
»That's right, soldier,« he said.

Henzel's word is law!

Monto put on the knuckleduster and took a step closer to Koto.
»I can help you find your uncle ...« Koto said under his breath. But Monto had already made up his mind.

In one swift move Monto took off the knuckleduster and threw it in the other soldier's face. The man went over backwards, knocking Henzel to the floor in his fall.

Henzel was gasping as he pushed the unconscious soldier away and got to his feet. Monto had already cut the ropes that held Koto. Henzel's metal claw clattered to the floor.

»Where do you think you're going?!« hissed Henzel and drew his rapier. The pain had exhausted Koto, but still he managed to grab the metal claw, parry the attack – and jab the claw into Henzel's leg.

I just risked my life for you!

Let's get out of here!

»Not without my taynikma,« said Koto, grabbing the odd object. Henzel was still screaming on the floor trying desperately to tear the claw from his leg.

Netherville

They ran this way!

Monto and Koto peered cautiously out from the shadows.

»We're lucky they didn't have a crystal like yours,« smiled Koto. Monto looked at the lantern in his belt.

»There are just a few of them in all of Tayclania,« said Monto. »It was a reward to my father for his heroic deeds in the corps!«

Monto sighed and shook his head.

»Thank you for saving my life,« said Koto.

I'm lawless now. A disgrace to my father!

»Nonsense!« said Koto. »You're a hero! And now we'll go look for your uncle!«

»We don't know where he is …«

»Not yet,« said Koto and pressed a button on top of the taynikma. A small lid opened and a strange blue light flickered underneath it. »A 'shadow pocket',« said Koto with a smile.

»What the …?!« said Monto as Koto held up the weird thing he had pulled out of the taynikma.

»It can hide any object. That's why the soldiers didn't find what I had taken from your uncle's house …«

»You stole that thing from my uncle?! Give it back!« said Monto. He tried to snatch the thing from Koto, but it fell from his hand. It rolled off the roof and they both jumped swiftly to the street.

What is that thing?!

»They call it a 'pathfinder',« said Koto. »It's an old nikma from the time of the clans. Master Gekko showed me a drawing of it. It will ...«

A nikma?
They've been
illegal for a
century!

»Why would Uncle Barto have one of those?«

»It will show you the way to a certain place,« continued Koto. »If your uncle had ever had to flee, it would show his allies the way to the clans ...«

»That thing can show us the way to my uncle?« asked Monto. »How?«

»I don't know,« said Koto. »Pathfinders were made so that only the right people could work them. That's why we have to get this one to Master Gekko quickly. He must know how to start it, and make it show the way to your uncle – or wherever it was meant to take you.«

Monto picked up the nikma ...

Monto was so shocked he dropped the thing once again. »What's going on?« he asked.

Koto looked just as surprised as the small beetle-like thing began walking around on its mechanical legs.

»I guess your uncle made you one of those 'right people' ...« said Koto and looked at Monto. »Now you just need to make it lead the way.«

Monto and Koto ran all they could.

They had to run fast to keep up with the small mechanical beetle. It led them to the old, ramshackle parts of Klanaka. A filthy slum housing only beggars and outcasts.

Phew! Did they have to make them to go so fast?!

»This way! Quick!« yelled Monto and pulled Koto inside the old house.

No one lived there and it looked as if it could collapse any moment.

»Where did the beetle go?« asked Koto and looked around.

»We'll find it,« said Monto and took out his lantern again.

Koto stayed away from the strong light.

Right there!

The nikma stood on the edge of a well.

Blast!!

Monto and Koto looked down into the vast darkness. It seemed like a bottomless pit.

Do we have to go down there?

»We can't,« snapped Monto. »We don't have any rope. Even if we did, I don't know what we'd tie it to!«

»Don't worry,« smiled Koto. »If you put away that crystal, I will get us some rope.« Monto shut off the lantern, and Koto stuck his hand into the shadows. »TENE-GARA!« he yelled and pulled a sticky, dark rope from the shadows.

Monto stared at Koto in disbelief but the shadow rope seemed perfectly strong. Koto began climbing down the rope and Monto followed right behind him.

Easy now.

We'll reach the bottom soon. It looks dry.

It was pitch black, but Koto obviously had perfect night vision. Finally Monto could feel the ground beneath his feet.

»Where are we?« asked Monto as he held on to Koto's sleeve.

»It looks like a tunnel,« answered Koto. »Follow me, but be very quiet!« They crept on and after a while Monto could see a light.

Koto walked slowly out of the tunnel while he looked around in awe.

»Watch out!« said Monto.

A trapdoor flung open with a sharp crack and Monto had to grab Koto by the neck to keep him from falling into a hole in the ground.

»Very quiet, eh?« whispered Monto. »Nice going – for a master thief!«

»I'm still just an apprentice,« growled Koto.

»WHO GOES?« sounded a deep voice behind them. »Only clan members are allowed inside Netherville!«

Where did you get a pathfinder?

And how did you turn it on?

»Where is Uncle Barto?« asked Monto and walked up to the burly man. »I want to see him now!«

The other men began whispering, but the burly man made them stop with a wave of his hand. He looked carefully at the young soldier.

»Are you Monto?« he asked.

Monto was so surprised by the man's words that he forgot his anger for a moment.

»Do you ... know me?« asked Monto and looked into the eyes of the man.

»Your uncle often spoke about you,« said the man.

My name is Arkin!

I am head of the Mountain Clan!

Monto hesitated, but finally he shook Arkin's big hand. »I am Monto. And this is Koto, apprentice of Master Gekko. He helped me find the way here ...«

Master GEKKO?!

Hmmpf!

»He betrayed the rebel clans many years ago. What would he send his errand boy for now?«

»I'm no errand boy!« said Koto, sending Arkin a sulky glance. »I am on a mission to find Monto's uncle. Master Gekko wants to see him ...«

»They found out what he was doing,« said Arkin in a bitter voice. »Now they will try to make him tell the way to Netherville. He's held in The Tower of the Sun!«

The Tower of the Sun?

Henzel's most terrible prison!

»A cruel place. Run by the evil Lt. Lenzor!«

»Lenzor? Evil?! That's not true!« protested Monto. »He might be tough, but he's fair. He's an honourable soldier!«

»You've been told many lies, Monto,« said Arkin. »You have a lot to learn ...«

I'll find the truth myself!

»Just tell me the way to that tower and I will free my uncle on my own!«

»Not without my help!« said Koto, smiling at Monto.

The Tower of the Sun

The sun was rising as Monto and Koto arrived in the small, hidden valley south of Klanaka. Arkin had given them a horse, and Koto had clung nervously to Monto all the way. He didn't like horses much.

»There it is,« said Monto and pointed. The tower glittered in the sun. Koto winced from the strong light.

We can't get any closer. They'll spot us a mile away!

How are we going to get in?!

»Through the gates, of course!« said Monto as he dismounted from the horse. He pulled Koto with him and took a piece of rope from the saddlebags.

»What makes you think they'll let us in?« sighed Koto, but Monto simply began tying up Koto's hands.

»A soldier from the corps arriving with an important prisoner ...« said Monto with a smile. »Why wouldn't they let us in?«

»OPEN THE GATES!« yelled the guard and the heavy iron grille slowly began to rise above their heads.

The chief is in the red barrack!

Monto simply nodded and rode inside the tower with Koto walking behind him. Far above them they could see the inside of the strange dome on top of the tower.

Fearsome, ghoulish guards were walking back and forth between the small cages, poking at the starving prisoners.

»Uncle Barto!« gasped Monto suddenly.

Monto jumped off the horse and stared at one of the cages. The man inside was in better shape than most of the other prisoners, but he had been beaten badly. Dark patches of dried blood covered parts of the many tattoos on his naked torso.

Easy now!

Don't draw their attention!

»We've found him. Might as well strike now,« whispered Monto. »You distract the guards while I get Uncle Barto out of that cage!«

Koto was about to protest, but Monto had already cut him loose.

»Run to the gates, Koto!« said Monto. »It will only take me a moment to free my uncle!«

Koto sighed, but did as he was told.

Stop him! He got out!

»Get him alive and unharmed!« yelled Monto.

»TENE-SORA!« said Koto as two guards tried to cut him off. A whip made of shadow appeared from the taynikma, and with a sharp crack Koto knocked them off their feet. Suddenly every guard was running towards him – and Monto could get to Barto's cage unnoticed.

Wake up,
Uncle!

Monto pulled the padlock. »You have to get out!«

»Monto?!« gasped Barto and looked up with weary eyes. His lips were completely dry and his skin was badly burnt form the sun.

»OPEN THE DOME!« a voice cried out from the red barrack.

Koto screamed in pain as beams of sun crushed his shadow shield and knocked him to the ground.

The light was blinding and Monto could just barely see Koto lying unmoving. »Hang on, Barto!« said Monto. He pulled out his mace and ran towards the guards that were closing in on Koto.

The creatures seemed totally unaffected by the powerful sunlight.

The heat was already unbearable. Each time Monto swung his mace he simply got more and more exhausted. He tried to keep on fighting, but it was a losing battle. Monto fell to his knees and a guard raised his weapon, ready to deal Monto the final blow.

»Stop!« sounded a stern voice. Monto could barely look up to see who spoke. »Cage the shadow boy!«

I'll take care of the renegade soldier ...

»Lt. Lenzor ...« gasped Monto just as he passed out from exhaustion.

SPLASH! The ice-cold water woke Monto. He was sitting in a chair in a small barrack. The shutters were closed and a couple of oil lamps lit up the room.

Monto wiped the water from his face – and realized his hands weren't tied.

Welcome, Monto!

»You're a brave lad,« said Lenzor as he poured himself a glass of wine. »But now it's time to teach you about your purpose in life. I'm giving you a chance. Your final chance ...«

Monto was silent for a while. »What kind of place is this?« Monto finally asked.

»The Tower of the Sun,« said Lenzor proudly. »A marvellous building. The ingenious pulley system enables us to open the dome on top of the tower. Then the sunlight is reflected and enhanced by the crystals – turning the yard into a burning desert!«

What for ...?

After a few days in The Tower of the Sun even the most hardened man will speak.

If he is still alive ...

»You ARE evil!« yelled Monto and jumped out of the chair and quickly grabbed a bottle from the table. He was about to strike out at Lenzor, but the three guards already had him surrounded.

»Calm down! We've had enough fighting today,« said Lenzor. »Guards – leave me alone with this boy. He's just got a bit of sunstroke ...«

The guards reluctantly withdrew and left the barrack. Monto gave Lenzor a suspicious look.

»What do you want from me?« asked Monto. He was still holding the bottle. »Why is Barto a prisoner?«

»He will have to lead us to the city of the rebel clans,« answered Lenzor and offered Monto a glass of wine. »I simply want to help him see the light ...«

There was a sudden change to Lenzor's expression. A sad look came into his face.

»My father's deathbed?!« said Monto and felt a sharp sting in his chest.

»I owe your father my life,« said Lenzor and looked away. »Did you know your father died in my arms?«

Protect my son!

Those were his final words ...

Lenzor put down the glass and gave a sigh.

»My father? He told you to ... protect me?« asked Monto, letting his arms fall. He was too confused now to attack Lenzor.

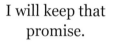

I will keep that promise.

But you have to follow orders!

You have your father's strength and courage. You could be an even greater soldier than he was!

»I don't want to be a soldier in an army of murderers and torturers,« said Monto with scorn.

»We're fighting scum! They're not like us, Monto,« said Lenzor and put his hand on Monto's shoulder. »You have to choose sides. Obey our leader or be our enemy!«

Monto didn't know what to say. Had his father really wanted him to follow Henzel blindly? Had he even known a place like this terrible tower existed?

»I will choose sides,« said Monto after a long silence. Lenzor nodded and with a sigh of relief he turned around to take his seat again – but as soon as he faced the other way, Monto smashed the bottle against the back of his head!

»I'm sorry, Lenzor,« said Monto. »Henzel is no longer my leader!«

»The sunlight is too strong,« thought Monto, as he stepped outside through the back door. He looked up at the merciless beams that shone through the giant crystals. The guards inside the yard were walking about, unaffected by the strong heat. »They must be some kind of desert creatures. I don't stand a chance against them as long as the dome is open ...«

Long, sturdy chains hung down from the dome to a large machine behind the barracks.

That must be the pulley system!

Monto crept over to the machine.

»I have to shut that dome,« thought Monto.

He spotted a metal rod on the ground. He snatched it up quickly.

»What is going on here?« said someone behind Monto, just as one of the chains jumped off a metal wheel and the dome began to close. Monto turned to see three guards staring straight at him.

»Don't panic ...« thought Monto. »You can still trick them!«

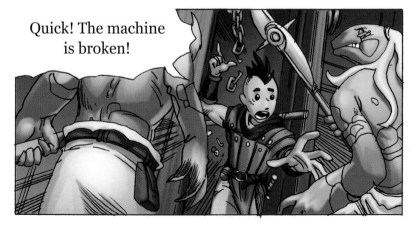

»Let's hope they fell for that,« he thought.

»I tried to fix it with the metal rod, but it didn't work!« said Monto. One of the guards began shouting orders to the two others.

»I have to get Koto and Barto out of their cages before the guards find Lenzor ...« thought Monto.

As the guards desperately tried to stop the machine from coming apart he got away into the yard. The dome was almost shut.

Koto!
Uncle Barto!

»What is going on?« asked Koto half asleep.

»We have to get out of here quickly!« said Monto.

He tried to pry open the padlock, but it was far too strong.

»Don't worry. I can open that lock!« said Koto and smiled at Monto.

I just need
my taynikma!
Where is it?

Your taynikma?!

It's our
only chance
of escaping!

Suddenly it hit Monto. Koto's things had been lying on the table inside the red barrack. Lenzor's barrack.

»I'll get you the taynikma,« said Monto and hurried back to the red building. He just had to hope Lenzor hadn't been found yet. There was plenty of yelling and shouting behind the barrack by the machine, and Monto could easily slip inside through the front door.

There were no guards inside. And no Lenzor!

Monto looked around quickly but Lenzor was not to be seen anywhere inside the room.

»I don't have time to look for him now,« thought Monto – just as he spotted the taynikma on the table, alongside his own mace and Koto's thief's gear. He grabbed it and headed for the door.

Where are you going?

Lenzor was still bleeding and he looked dazed, but Monto knew he would still be able to fire the crossbow. And hit his target!

»I'm sorry I had to hit you on the head, Lenzor,« said Monto. »But I don't want to be in your army!«

»I swore, Monto!« said Lenzor. »I promised your father I would protect you. Don't make me kill you!«

»Kill me?! Why?« gasped Monto.

He could feel his legs tremble. »Just let me go,« continued Monto. »All I wanted was to help my uncle. He's the only family I have left!«

We all have to follow our destiny, Monto ...

Monto was paralyzed by fear. His feet were stuck to the floor like glue and he couldn't look away from Lenzor's sad gaze.

TCHUNK! The bolt from the crossbow slammed right into the door behind Monto. »Run,« said Lenzor and lowered the crossbow. »Run fast ...«

Monto was totally confused, but he didn't have time to ask any questions.

He just had to get the taynikma to Koto. Monto gave Lenzor one last look – then he ran!

Monto rushed back out to the cage.

I found it!

The shadow powers were already sending sparks flying and as soon as Koto put it on he regained his strength and willpower.

Let me show you what a moon-pick can do ...

Within a heartbeat Koto had unlocked the cage – and it was not a moment too soon! »The guards are coming!« gasped Uncle Barto as Monto and Koto pulled him from the cage. Four of the desert creatures were just about to attack with their deadly spears.

»We'll have to fight our way out!« yelled Monto and swung his mace. »Find a weapon, Koto. QUICK!«

»Don't worry,« said Koto. »I have my weapons here!«

TENE-SORA!

They are weak
without the sunlight!
Get them!

Monto and Koto were strong enough to beat back the guards, but they still had to get out.

»We need horses,« said Monto. »Uncle Barto is too weak to run!«

Monto and Koto carried Barto over to the stables right by the outer gates.

»Faster! They're closing the gates!« yelled Koto.

As Monto passed Koto he grabbed him by the wrist and pulled him up from the ground. »We're off!« Koto held on to Monto as best he could.

Monto was a skilled rider and the guards had no chance of catching up. They reached Klanaka and took Uncle Barto with them back to Netherville.

»I doubt Barto would have lived through another day in that evil tower!«

»I couldn't have done it without Koto,« said Monto and pointed proudly at his friend.

Arkin grumbled and gave Koto a suspicious look.

Monto was surprised by Arkin's words. Didn't they trust Koto?

»Koto is my friend,« said Monto and pushed Arkin's hand away from his shoulder. »And he fought just as bravely as I to save Uncle Barto!«

But he's not one of us!

Not one of us?

The last person I heard talk like that was Lt. Lenzor!

»Don't get clever with me, Monto!« said Arkin and was just about to slap Monto ...

»STOP!« said a weak, but strong-willed voice. Barto had gotten to his feet and stepped in front of Arkin. »You big oaf! Do you think I risked my life just so that you could continue the ridiculous clan feuds? Who's going to stop Henzel, if we spend our time fighting each other?«

Arkin looked very surprised and obviously didn't know what to say.

Barto took a small package from a chest.

»Only by joining forces will the clans be able to defeat Henzel,« said Barto. Arkin was just about to say something, but then he changed his mind. With a sheepish look he finally offered Koto his hand.

»Thank you for your help,« he said. »You are always welcome among us, Koto ...«

»And you, Monto,« said Barto and held out the package. »You proved yourself worthy to be a warrior of the Mountain Clan. This heirloom has been waiting for you to choose your true destiny!«

What is it?

The Mountain Taynikma!

See what happens in Book 4: **The Lost Catacombs**

Th-there's something down there ...

Readers' Pages

Welcome to your own Taynikma pages! This is where we bring drawings and greetings from other Taynikma readers.

Send in your drawings or write to us with your questions. If we publish your contribution we will send the book to you free of charge!

Reader Drawings
Yacub Jamhin , 10 years, and Ruby Hillman, 8 years, have made these fine drawings of Koto.

Sneak gets buried in boxes

Sangeeta, 6 years.

In Book 2: **"The Rats"** there is a dramatic scene where Koto uses his shadow power to pull a stack of boxes over Sneak. Sangeeta Mishra used her imagination and came up with this drawing of how it looked when the boxes fell on top of Sneak

Reader Question

"Hey Taynikma! In Book 2: **"The Rats"** I noticed how Koto's eyes change colour. When he jumps down into the Rats' Nest they have turned red and in the next picture they are blue again. Why do Koto's eyes change colour?"

Answer

Well spotted. Koto has blue eyes but when he uses his shadow power to see in the dark, his eyes are a glowing red! It happened the first time in Book 1: **Master Thief.** Can you find the picture?

Send your drawings and greetings to:

Taynikma
PO Box 6268
London W1A 2HE
mail@taynikma.co.uk

59

Hands

Most beginners have a hard time drawing hands and usually they will try to hide them like this:

Art school

You can't keep doing tricks like that if you want to be a real artist some day.

Here are three facts that will make it easier for you to draw hands:

1. The length of a hand:

A hand is as long as the distance between your chin and your forehead.

2. The length of your fingers:

You can split a hand in two equal size boxes. One will be the fingers and the other the palm of the hand. Our longest finger is as long as the palm.

Notice how the thumb reaches the first part of the index finger.

3. Fingers meet in one point:

If you spread your fingers they will all point towards the same point in your wrist. Look at your own hand.

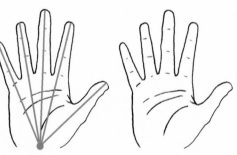

See? There's no excuse for not practicing how to draw hands. After all they're right there at the end of your arms ...

Colouring

The drawings in Taynikma have been coloured on the computer. Here is how it works:

1. We scan the drawing on a scanner.

2. Then we do a so-called "colour test". In this picture from Book 1 Koto is on his first mission. We chose murky colours as he was under water at night.

3. Then the colourist makes what we call a "flat colouring". That means he takes the colours from the model sheet (remember those from Book 2), and places them on the figure in the picture.

That way you know you have all the right basic colours in all the right places.

4. Finally you grade the colours to look like the colour test – and then you add shadows and highlights. The final picture looks like this:

TAYNIKMA is a series of ten books!
Follow the adventures of Koto here:

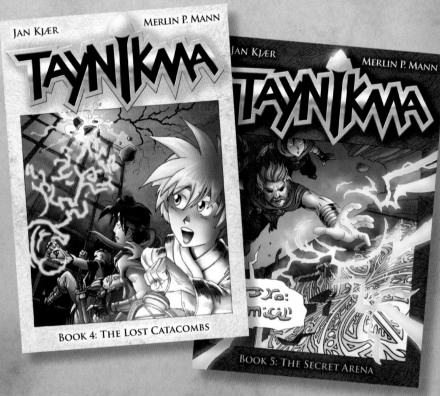

Books 1 - 4 are available already
Book 5 will be out soon
- ask at your local book store or shop online

Check for news and updates on our website
www.taynikma.co.uk